Matters of

VIDEO GAMES

By
Hayley Mitchell Haugen

NORWOOD HOUSE PRESS
CHICAGO, ILLINOIS

Norwood House Press
P.O. Box 316598
Chicago, Illinois 60631

For information regarding Norwood House Press, please visit our website at:
www.norwoodhousepress.com or call 866-565-2900.

Hardcover ISBN: 978-1-59953-601-9   Paperback ISBN: 978-1-60357-581-2

LIBRARY OF CONGRESS CATALOGING-IN-PUBLICATION DATA

Haugen, Hayley Mitchell, 1968-
 Video games / by Hayley Mitchell Haugen.
   pages cm. -- (Matters of opinion)
 Includes bibliographical references and index.
 Summary: "Explores the pros and cons of several issues related to video
games, including whether video games cause violence, discourage exercise,
and proper regulation. Aligns with Common Core Language Arts Anchor
Standards for Reading Informational Text and Speaking and Listening. Text
contains critical thinking components in regards to social issues and
history. Includes bibliography, glossary, index, and relevant websites"--
Provided by publisher.
  ISBN 978-1-59953-601-9 (library edition : alk. paper) -- ISBN
978-1-60357-594-2 (ebook) 1. Video games--Social aspects--Juvenile
literature. I. Title.
  GV1469.34.S52H38 2014
  794.8--dc23
                          2014003798

310R—092017
Manufactured in the United States of America in East Peoria, Illinois.

Contents

Note: Words that are **bolded** in the text are defined in the glossary.

Timeline

1993 Senators Joseph Lieberman of Connecticut and Herbert Kohl of Wisconsin launch a Senate investigation into violence in video games, hoping to initiate a ban on violent games.

1994 Resulting from the Senate investigation, the Entertainment Software Rating Board is created. Ratings on video game packaging now indicate the suggested age of players and the extent of violent content.

1995 The Sony PlayStation is released in the United States.

1997 Arizona proposes a bill to restrict the distribution of violent video games to minors. The bill is not approved.

1998 Walmart bans from its stores more than 50 video games that it deems inappropriate for minors.

1999 On April 20, Littleton, Colorado, high school students Eric Harris and Dylan Klebold kill 12 peers and one teacher and wound 21 others during a shooting spree at Columbine High School. The perpetrators were video game players.

2001 The U.S. surgeon general's office releases a report that concludes media play only a small role in contributing to youth violence.

2008 Grand Theft Auto 4 breaks sales records its first week after gamers buy more than 6 million copies.

2010 The U.S. Supreme Court rules 7–2 that a law in California restricting the sale or rental of violent video games is unconstitutional.

2013 Grand Theft Auto 5 from Rockstar Games and Take-Two Interactive becomes the fastest-selling game in history.

1 What Are the Issues with Video Games?

In September 2013 Grand Theft Auto 5 (GTA 5) came out. It was a joint release from Rockstar Games and Take-Two Interactive. Loyal fans had been looking forward to the game. They bought nearly 28 million copies in the first three weeks of its launch. Strauss Zelnick is CEO of Take-Two. He said that the game's launch was "one for the record books." He called it "the fastest selling entertainment release in history."[1] It made sales of $3 billion in three days.

The sales of GTA 5 show how popular video games are. They are a big industry. They make billions of dollars in profits. Nintendo sold more than 6.47 million pieces of 3DS software in 2013. Luigi's Mansion: Dark Moon alone sold 863,000 copies.

Video games like Grand Theft Auto are very popular in the United States, where gun violence is higher than in Europe or Canada. Whether playing video games contributes to gun violence, however, has never been proven.

XBOX 360

NTSC

grand theft auto FIVE

SEPTEMBER 17

🐦 #GTAV

RATING PENDING
RP

Video Games Make Money, but Does That Make Them Good?

Video games are a big part of the economy. But not everyone accepts them. Many have raised concerns about them. This includes parents, teachers, doctors, and politicians. They worry about the health and safety of youth. Kids are the main players of video games. People ask whether this latest craze is a good thing. They ask whether it will have long-lasting bad effects.

One of the most common questions raised about video games is what effect the games have on young players. Advances in video games have helped designers create

? Did You Know

Parents Monitor Gamers

Parents are present when games are purchased or rented 91 percent of the time.

The most common questions raised about video games is what effect the games have on young players.

very realistic games. The bloody zombies in House of the Dead are just one example. They are scary. Players can hunt the creatures from the realistic **first-person perspective** of a character in the game. They feel that they are living in the game. And they are about to be eaten!

Critics say that the Grand Theft Auto video games are meant for adult players — they are too violent for young players.

Games-like-these.com says first-person shooter games are popular. It is fun for gamers to be thrown right into the action of the games. "Those who play them understand the adrenaline rush of being equipped with the latest futuristic weapons and using them to save the

Did You Know

There Are Good Reasons Why People Play Video Games

Anupam Jolly is a writer. In 2013 he wrote an article called "Why Do People Play Video Games." In it he says there is not just one answer to this question. He says that people play video games because they are fun. He notes that "playing video games offers a constant source of learning." He also says that people play video games for a sense of achievement. "While in the real world, feeling that sense requires a lot, in video games, a player can easily get that adrenaline rush to achieve something."

Anupam Jolly, "Why Do People Play Video Games?," www.why.do, March 18, 2013.

Earth. While they may not be the most politically correct games and they may include graphic violence and all manner of strange creatures engineered in the minds of the developers, there is no doubt that they are a lot of fun."[2]

Women Play, Too!

Forty-two percent of all game players are women. In fact, 37 percent of gamers are women over the age of 18. Boys the age of 17 or younger make up only 13 percent of gamers.

GTA 5 is not a first-person shooter game. But the game lets players make characters steal cars, rob citizens, and beat up or kill others. Chris Suellentrop writes for the *New York Times*. He wrote about the newest version of the game. He says it is "still an action game about hoodlums and thieves; we start with an extended bout of cop killing and proceed to a series of increasingly ambitious heists."[3] Critics think it is too violent for young players. The game is clearly made for adult players. But adults are not the only ones who play it. The concern is that some kids spend a lot of time playing violent video games. And they may become violent themselves. Some researchers think that gamers may enjoy the pretend violence of these games so much that they use real violence to solve their problems.

These fears have grown worse. This is because first-person shooter games have become more real looking. The games also make players feel like they are really shooting.

These fears have also been fueled by many mass shootings. Some of these were done by violent video game players. One of these was Adam Lanza. In 2012

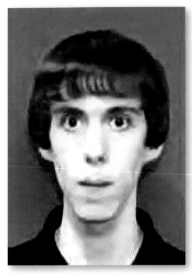

Adam Lanza was a video gamer who went on a real shooting spree.

he went on a shooting spree at Sandy Hook Elementary School in Newtown, Connecticut. He killed 20 first-graders and six adults.

Another Issue with Video Games

Violence is a big concern with video games. But another issue with the topic is how it affects health. Children as young as two are now playing video games. By the time children are teenagers, they have spent much of their life playing them. The time people spend on video games each year is going up. In 2002 Americans 12 and over played 71 hours per year. By 2012 they were playing 142 hours.

Many experts worry that as children spend more time indoors playing games, they miss out. They stop playing outside. They stop engaging with friends and family. They also spend a lot less time playing sports, running, or biking. Not only do children spend less time outdoors playing, they tend to eat more snacks when they play video games. A lack of active play in addition to snacking may be increasing obesity. Obesity in children is a serious problem. And many in the health field think playing video games may be to blame.

A Look Inside This Book

The video games debate is complex. In this book, three of the issues will be covered in more detail: Do video games create violence in society? Are video games bad for our health? Should violent video games be regulated? Each chapter ends with a section called **Examine the Opinions**, which highlights one argumentative technique used in the chapter. At the end of the book, students can test their skills at writing their own essay on the book's topic. Finally, notes, glossary, a bibliography and an index provide additional resources.

2 Do Video Games Create Violence in Society?

 Yes: Video Games Cause Violent Behavior

In 2012 Charlotte Bacon was in kindergarten. On December 14 she left home and went to Sandy Hook Elementary School. It was just like any other school day. But that day twenty-year-old Adam Lanza killed his mother at home. Then he went to Charlotte's school. He went on a shooting spree. Charlotte died at school that day by Lanza's hand. So did 19 of her classmates and six adults.

Afterward, the media debated a number of issues. The gun Lanza used in his attack was easy to get. Was this to blame? Or was it the influence of violent video games in his life? News reports focused on his "obsession" for violent video games such as Call of Duty. This is a first-

A scene from Call of Duty.

person shooter game. It takes place during World War II. One reporter said that the game let the shy boy's "lust for slaughter [jump] from his TV screen to real life."[4]

Violent Games Create Violent Children

Some people say violent video games make people violent. They claim first-person shooting games make violence look fun. They make violence in real life seem normal. It is no wonder, they say, that mass shooters play violent video games.

Steven F. Gruel is a lawyer. In 2010 he went before the California Supreme Court. He argued about violent video games. He said that the state had the right to restrict the sale of these games to kids. He said the games should only be played by adults. Gruel cited a 2006 Federal Trade Commission study. It said that 70 percent of 13- to 16-year-olds are able to buy Mature, or M-rated, games. He says this is a problem. It "lets gamers [virtually] murder, burn, and maim law

Contains strong
bloody violence

18

©2002

Suitable only for persons of 18 years and over
Not to be supplied to any person below that age.

A warning that appears on a video game. The label also specifies age requirements.

enforcement officers, racial minorities, and members of clergy as well as sexually assault women."[5]

Gruel also cited the results of more than 130 studies. These were found in journals such as *Pediatrics*. The studies helped support his view. They showed that violent video games have an effect on kids. He said the studies showed that playing such games "increases aggressive

Children See Too Much Violence in Video Games

Many groups have concerns about video game violence. One of these is the Lion and Lamb Project. This group worries about the amount of violence kids see in these games. It looked at boys aged 8 to 18. It found that they will see up to 124 acts of violence every 10 minutes they play these games. That number is even higher for games rated Teen or Mature. In those, players will see more than 180 violent acts every 40 minutes. That adds up to 5,400 violent acts a month.

Violent scenes are a frequent occurrence in video games.

The California Supreme Court building.

thought and behavior; increases antisocial behavior and delinquency; engenders poor school performance; and desensitizes the game player to violence."[6]

The case went all the way to the U.S. Supreme Court, which ruled against Gruel. It did not restrict the sale of violent video games. The court said it was unconstitutional to do so. Gruel and many politicians, teachers, and parents still want more regulation of violent games.

But Not So Fast...

 No: There Is No Proof That Violent Video Games Lead to Violent Behavior

Many people claim violent video games make people act in violent ways. They cite studies to prove their claims. Others say the facts do not support this view. Criminals may play violent video games. But this does not prove that video games are the cause of their bad behavior. Christopher Ferguson is a psychology professor. He says it is true that most school shooters have been young men who play violent video games. But he says most young men play video games today. And most of them do not commit violent crimes. He says that males play more violent games than females do. Males are also more aggressive. So of course, he says, there will be a link between these games and aggression. But there will also be a link between "aggression and growing beards,

Violent Video Games Do Not Harm Mentally Healthy Youth

Patrick and Charlotte Markey are professors. They looked at what effect video games have on teens. They found that it depends on the teens' mental health. They say that "if a child is easily angered, prone to depression or generally [disobedient]," violent games may make these things worse. This means that only some kids may be violent after playing such games. Most kids do not respond badly to violent games. Christopher Ferguson says such games "are like peanut butter." He says they are harmless for most kids. But they can harm kids who already have mental health problems.

Otherwise, June 10, 2010.

participation in sports, wearing pants rather than skirts, and a preference for dating women—in short, anything else that is a male-dominated activity."[7]

People commit violent acts for many reasons. Lanza had a mental illness. It was untreated. This is more likely to have played a role in his violent acts than video games alone. One study in the British medical

Gamers playing video games. Not everyone believes violent video games lead to violent behavior.

journal *The Lancet* shows that violent acts are not caused by one thing. They are caused by many factors. These combine over time. The study found that video games are not a very big factor when it comes to youth violence. It says that bigger factors are "involvement in crime, poverty, family breakdown or abuse, drug use, and psychiatric illness."[8] In light of this, **advocates** for violent video games say that it is not fair to single them out as the cause of youth violence.

Closing Arguments

Violent events in American culture have caused people to wonder whether violent video games are to blame. Could violent games be creating violent children? Some groups use scientific studies to prove that they do. On the other hand, other groups claim that these studies are not conclusive. Violence, they say, is caused by many sociological and psychological factors. Violent video games cannot be blamed.

Examine the Opinions

Evaluate the Author's Credibility

Essay writers know to back up their claims. They include facts, statistics, and opinions. Every argument has a **counterargument**. This is the other side. Research has not proved that violent games turn mentally healthy kids into criminals. But some still claim there is a connection. Whom should you believe? When looking at the arguments of others, think about who they are. Is the author an expert in the field? What does he or she have to gain by arguing one way or another for an issue? For example, Gruel argued in court for restrictions on video game sales. He seems like a good source. He is a lawyer. Readers can assume he is an educated person. On the other hand, readers may wonder what he has to gain from taking on this topic. Maybe he has job-related reasons for joining the video game debate. But Gruel refers to two studies in his argument. The Federal Trade Commission and *Pediatrics* are both well-known, reliable sources. Many readers will feel that they can trust Gruel because he backs up his arguments with trustworthy sources. Trustworthy sources help provide the evidence needed to support any convincing argument.

3 Are Video Games Bad for Our Health?

 Yes: Video Games Are Unhealthy

People do not agree on the issue of whether video games lead to obesity and other health-related problems. Some kids have stopped playing outdoors. They do not get enough exercise. Some have even stopped reading books. Instead, they play video games. If this keeps up, people worry that America will end up with a fat, uneducated society.

The American Obesity Association says more than 30 percent of kids aged 6 to 19 are overweight. And more than 15 percent are obese. This can lead to health problems later in life. It can cause heart disease, diabetes, and stroke. Alexandra Momyer is a fitness trainer. She

Some think there is a link between video games and obesity.

says there is a link between video games and obesity. She says when kids play such games, "they are likely to increase their snacking and food intake, and they are also more prone to make unhealthy food choices. This [makes] weight gain more likely."[9] Parents and doctors

TV and Video Games May Cause Obesity

A 2010 study of children in Switzerland indicated that video games, along with other sitting-down activity, was linked to obesity. According to Nicolas Stettler, M.D., a pediatric nutrition specialist at the Children's Hospital of Philadelphia: "To our knowledge this study provides the strongest evidence for an independent association between time spent playing electronic games and childhood obesity. Our findings suggest that the use of electronic games should be limited to prevent childhood obesity."

Abigale Elise, "Do Video Games Lead to Obesity?," February 2, 2010. www.health.am.

fear that because of video games, kids are no longer riding bikes. They fear kids have stopped playing sports or spending time outdoors.

Video games may lure kids away from healthy mental activities, too. This includes reading. In 2011 the *Chattanooga Times* said that many teens have stopped reading. They would rather play video games. The

Many teens stop reading when they start playing video games.

paper said, "The result of this societal shift is predictable. Reading test scores are dropping and the number of teens who read regularly for recreation is falling." A big concern is that these non-reading gamers will miss out on the chance to "make better grades, obtain higher levels of education, and fare better in the job market."[10]

But Not So Fast...

 NO: Video Games Can Be Good for Us

Most video game advocates agree that people should not spend all their time on video games. But they also say that these games can be good for people. They foster critical thinking. They help with problem-solving skills. They help kids get active in phys ed classes. And many people turn to video game exercise programs at home to keep fit. Doctors even prescribe video game therapy for some patients.

David Katz is director of the Prevention Research Center. He points out that today's active video games help kids get exercise. He quotes a study that says kids "burn more than four times as many calories per minute playing an active video game than playing a seated game, and their heart rate is also significantly higher with the active game."[11]

Video Games Do Not Cause Obesity

Matt Peckham writes for *PC World*. He cited a study from Michigan State University. He said it shows video games may not be to blame for obesity in kids. He says these games had no more effect on weight gain than using the Internet or cell phones. In fact, he said, the study showed the biggest factors were "race, age, and socioeconomic status." These games may not make gamers gain weight.

Matt Peckham, "Study: Video Games Do Not Make You Fat, Just Dumb and Depressed," *PC World*, January 21, 2011.

People worry that video games have replaced books. They fear the games do not help kids learn good thinking skills. But a 2011 study looked at nearly 500 12-year-olds in Michigan. It found that video games may foster creative skills in boys and girls. Linda Jackson was the head of the project. She says, "Not only are (video games) not all bad, there's some 'intellectual' good to be found in playing them. We [found] that no other technologies except video games was positively related to creativity."[12]

Some of today's games involve physical activity and exercise, which helps fight obesity.

Studies have found video games may help in other ways, too. Mark Griffiths is director of the International Gaming Research Unit. He says that these games can give some a sense of release after a bad day. He says,

"When you have done really well in a game, you feel good—and that raises one's self-esteem. Video games are wonderful [ways to forget your problems]."[13]

These games can also help people with physical or psychological problems. Randolf Palmaira is director of a nursing center in New York. He says that video games

Nintendo demonstrates their new game "Wii Fit" in Japan. The game uses a balance board to help people exercise with yoga, hula hoops, and push-ups.

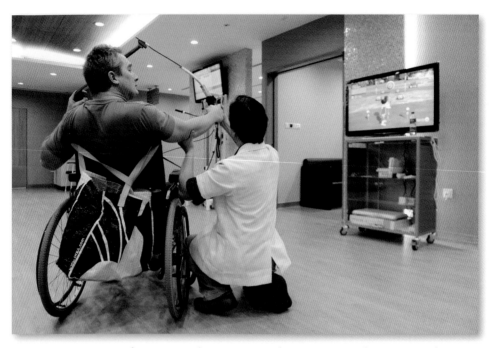

A man recovering from a stroke uses a video game in therapy. Video games can help people who are ill or disabled.

are used in therapy to treat phobias. These include fear of heights and public speaking. They are also used to treat addictions to alcohol and drugs. His patients like playing games such as car racing and soccer. He says the games are more fun than "a traditional exercise for hip replacement patients of stepping up and down on a staircase. Which activity would you prefer?"[14]

Closing Arguments

Are video games bad for us, or are they actually helpful? People do not agree. Some people argue that video game playing leads to obesity in children. Kids who spend too much time playing video games do not do other physically or mentally healthy things. Other people say that video games can help kids improve their critical thinking skills. Some games even encourage kids to exercise, and they can be helpful as therapy for injured or disabled people.

Examine the Opinions

Recognizing Deceptive Arguments

People may never agree on whether there are more benefits to video games than drawbacks. As you read arguments about video games, note the ways authors try to sway you. Some try to appeal to readers' sense of **logic**, **ethics**, or emotion. The *Chattanooga Times* reported that teens read less often. It said reading test scores are falling. This author is appealing to the readers' emotions. The writer is using a **scare tactic** to get their attention. The appeal is strong. Most people agree that lower reading scores are not a good thing. The problem here is that the author does not make a logical connection in this argument. He or she does not use any statistics or facts to prove that the drop in scores is related to video games. Teens may be playing sports or doing volunteer work instead of reading in their spare time. Watch out! Some authors use emotional appeals when they do not have enough hard evidence to support their argument. The strongest writers strive for a balance between logical, ethical, and emotional appeals in their work. When all three of these appeals are working together, readers are less likely to question a writer's opinion on a topic.

4 Should Violent Video Games Be Regulated?

 Yes: Violent Video Games Need to Be Regulated

There are many arguments against violent video games. These arguments have led some to think that sales of these games should be regulated by the government, or even banned outright. These people believe that playing violent video games can cause real-life violence. Parents alone cannot be responsible for keeping them away from their children, only laws can. One mother who posted on Debate.org seconds this opinion: "The reason why I say that violent video games should be banned is because they are meant for adults, not children. It is impossible for the game creators to enforce their M rated games.... In today's society, adults are too busy doing their own things and don't have the time to monitor their children, leaving them to develop on their own."[15]

Video games can be bought in stores or online.

Common Sense

Many people think that it is just common sense to keep children away from the graphic violence of video games. Children can become used to the violent acts they perform in shooting games, and no study needs to prove it. As blogger John Hinderaker claims, "I personally

The issue of banning violent video games has gone all the way to the supreme court. Justice Antonin Scalia (pictured) wrote the majority opinion.

never play video games, and care nothing about them. I think the violent ones are aesthetically appalling, morally repellent and a symptom of the degradation of our culture. I think the world would be a much better place without them, and I suspect that they contribute to violence." [16]

Society Needs to Regulate Violence

While some groups continue to debate governmental regulation issues surrounding video games, other groups believe that there are some issues that need to be regulated through society, not legislation. The editors for the *Press of Atlantic City*, for example, feel that the violence in video games has crossed a line that has nothing to do with censorship. They say these violent images "would have shocked and disgusted our grandparents." They say kids do not just watch this violence. "They are participants, deeply immersed in the experience." The editors say that it is up to adults to stop this. They must send a message to game designers about this material. The editors say we do not have to treat game designers like filmmakers. "And we don't have to make them rich by consuming their products."

Press of Atlantic City (NJ), "Editorial: A Culture of Violence—The Need to Change," December 23, 2012.

The state of California tried to ban the sale of violent video games to minors in 2011. But the U.S. Supreme Court struck down California's law. In order

Many video game purchases are made by parents. Some parents may not be as concerned with the rating system as others.

to quiet protests, however, video game companies chose to place ratings on their games to warn parents about violence. Today, all violent video games carry a rating. Video games are rated for specific ages, just like ratings on movies. The ratings are given by the ESRB, or Entertainment Software Rating Board. The ESRB is a private organization.

Jim Matheson is a congressman from Utah. He wrote the Video Games Ratings Enforcement Act. The bill says that video games must be labeled with ratings. It says stores may not sell mature games to kids under age 18. Matheson says the bill will give peace of mind to parents. They will know that kids cannot gain legal access to these games. Matheson says he is not trying to take away adults' rights to play mature games. He says that "parents deserve every resource available to evaluate programming to which their children might be exposed. This bill is designed to back parents up in their effort to protect their children from what the industry has labeled as violent and/or sexually explicit material."[17]

But Not So Fast...

No: Video Games Should Not Be Regulated

Just how well does the video game rating system work? These ratings are only useful if people understand them. They must make good use of them, too. Many parents do not think twice about taking teens to movies rated R. These same parents may buy their teens video games rated M (mature).

The Video Games Ratings Enforcement Act Is Censorship

Congress looked at a new bill. It was called the Video Games Ratings Enforcement Act. The bill said that all video games must have an ESRB (Entertainment Software Rating Board) rating on them. The bill is still pending. Mitch Bowman is a blogger. He thinks bills like this lead to censorship. He says they limit free expression. "The government is handing over the reins of moral judgment to a private corporation.... How can we be sure the ESRB represents the values of the majority of American citizens, when they're a private company with no accountability to the public?"

Mitch Bowman, "Censorship at Its Finest: H.R. 287, the 'Video Games Ratings Enforcement Act,'" *Transparent Seas* (blog), January 17, 2013.

Many parents do use the video game ratings. The Federal Trade Commission said in 2007 that "87% of parents surveyed said they are aware of the ESRB system; more than seven in ten use it when their child wants to play a game for the first time."[18]

Fernando Trujano says these ratings can do a good job of helping parents and teachers choose games for kids, but he is against a total ban. This is because video game sales in the United States reached $21 billion in 2011. He argues that "if they are banned the economy will dramatically fall."[19]

Video Game Ratings Do Not Always Keep Mature Games Away from Kids

Nadia Oxford is a writer and gamer. She does not think that the ESRB system works. She talked with Chang Liu. He used to work at a game store. His store required ID for the purchase of M-rated games, making it hard for kids under 18 to buy these games. Liu said that many parents just went with their kids to the store and bought the games for them. He says, "When they made M-rated purchases [they] did so without a fuss, though it was impossible to tell if they trusted their young children with

This is the ratings symbol that appears on a video game for ages 10+.

mature content, thought ESRB ratings were present for decoration, or didn't care."[20]

Oxford doubts the ESRB helps. She asks if it is "just a way to siphon a fee out of a developer's pocket in exchange for a letter that, some players feel, doesn't tell the whole story about the supposedly objectionable material in a game?"[21] She thinks the ratings are a good thing overall. But she feels they could be improved.

Closing Arguments

Opponents of violent video games who have tried to get them banned did not win their battle. The U.S. Supreme Court ruled that violent video games are protected under the constitutional right to free speech. Video game sales are now regulated, however, by the video game rating system. These restrictions help keep mature games created for adults out of the hands of youths. Still, people argue that the rating system is not doing enough because kids can still get these games.

Examine the Opinions

Logical Fallacies

Logical fallacies are errors in logic. Writers may make these errors on purpose. This is a way to trick readers into agreeing with them. Trujano said that the economy will "dramatically fall" if violent video games are banned. He made use of a **slippery slope** fallacy. This warns of extreme negative consequences. But it does not show how we get to those extremes. For example, video game sales do add to the economy, but the nation does not rely on these sales to thrive. Another thing to consider with authors' arguments is whether they give facts or only opinions in their work. Strong writers will explain how their views on an issue have been shaped by facts. Oxford gave her opinion when she said the ESRB system needed to be improved. But she backed this up with facts when she talked to Liu. Liu knows from experience that parents buy mature-rated games for their kids.

Wrap It Up!

Write Your Own Essay

In this book, the essays gave many opinions about video games. These opinions can be used to write your own short essay on video games. Short opinion essays are a common writing form. They are also a good way to use the ideas in this book. The author gave several argumentative techniques that can be used. Evaluating the author's credibility, recognizing deceptive arguments, and logical fallacy were techniques used in the essays to sway the reader. Any of these could be used in a piece of writing.

There are 6 steps to follow in writing an essay:

Step One: Choose a Topic

When writing your essay, first choose a topic. You can start with one of the three chapter questions from the table of contents in this book. Decide which side of the issue you will take.

Step Two: Choose Your Theme

After choosing your topic, use the materials in this book to write the thesis, or theme, of your essay. You can use the titles of the articles in this book or the sidebar titles as examples of themes. The first paragraph should state your theme. For example, in an essay titled "Violent Video Games Should Be Regulated," state your opinion. Say why you think video games harm users. You could also use a short anecdote, or story, that proves your point and will interest your reader.

Step Three: Research Your Topic

You will need to do some further research to find enough material for your topic. You can find useful books and articles to look up in the bibliography and the notes of this book. Be sure to cite your sources, using the notes at the back of this book, as an example.

Step Four: The Body of the Essay

In the next three paragraphs, develop this theme. To develop your essay, come up with three reasons why violent video games should be regulated. For example, three reasons could be:

- *Violent video games are often sold to underage gamers.*
- *First-person shooter games are so realistic that they desensitize real-life violence.*
- *Youths who play violent video games may be more likely to commit acts of violence.*

These three ideas should each be given their own paragraph. Be sure to give a piece of evidence in each paragraph. Your evidence could be a **testimonial** from a sociologist or a person who has been harmed by violent video games. By using a sociologist, you can establish that the testimonial is from a credible source. You could also use a logical fallacy, such as a scare tactic or a slippery slope argument to convince your reader of the urgency of the argument. Each paragraph should end with a transition sentence that sums up the main idea in the paragraph and moves the reader to the next.

Step Five: Writing Your Conclusion

The final, or fifth, paragraph should state your conclusion. This should restate your theme and sum up the ideas in your essay. It could also end with an engaging quote or piece of evidence that wraps up your essay!

Step Six: Review Your Work

Finally, be sure to reread your essay. Does it have quotes, facts, and/or anecdotes to support the conclusions? Are the ideas clearly presented? Have another reader take a look at it to see whether someone else can understand your ideas. Make any changes that you think can help make your essay better.

Congratulations on using the ideas in this book to write a personal essay!

Notes

Chapter 1: What Are the Issues with Video Games?

1. Quoted in Dave Neal, "Rockstar's GTA 5 Sells Almost 30 Million Copies," *Inquirer*, October 30, 2013. www.theinquirer.net/inquirer/news/2303803/rockstar-s-gta-5-sells-almost-30-million-copies?flv=1.

2. Games-like-these.com, "Best First Person Shooter Games for PC," November 2, 2013. www.games-like-these.com/best-first-person-shooter-games-for-pc.

3. Chris Suellentrop, "Grand Theft Auto V Is a Return to the Comedy of Violence," *New York Times*, September 16, 2013. www.nytimes.com/2013/09/17/arts/video-games/grand-theft-auto-v-is-a-return-to-the-comedy-of-violence.html?pagewanted%3Dall&_r=0.

Chapter 2: Do Video Games Create Violence in Society?

4. Edgar Sandoval, Dan Friedman, and Bill Hutchinson, "News Report on Sandy Hook Gunman Adam Lanza's Video Game–Style Slaughter Score Sheet Inspires Calls in DC to Stiffen Regulation of Violent Games," *New York Daily News*, March 18, 2013. www.nydailynews.com/news/national/crackdown-urged-violent-games-lanza-report-article-1.1292402#ixzz2jbALcb00.

5. Quoted in Noah Berlatsky, ed., *Media Violence*. Detroit, MI: Greenhaven, 2012.

6. Quoted in Berlatsky, *Media Violence*.

7. Christopher J. Ferguson, "Violent Video Games: Dogma, Fear, and Pseudoscience," *Skeptical Inquirer*, September/October 2009. www.tamiu.edu/~cferguson/skeptinq.pdf.

8. *Lancet*, "Is Exposure to Media Violence a Public Health Risk?," April 5, 2008. http://download.thelancet.com/pdfs/journals/lancet/PIIS014067360860495X.pdf.

Chapter 3: Are Video Games Bad for Our Health?

9. Alexandra Momyer, "Do Video Games Contribute to Childhood Obesity?," Livestrong.com, February 8, 2011. www.livestrong.com/article/376383-obesity-in-children-video-games/#ixzz2jc1fKL8T.

10. *Chattanooga (TN) Times/Free Press*, "Targeting Teen Readers," October 10, 2011. http://timesfreepress.com/news/2011/oct/10/targeting-teen-readers/?opiniontimes.

11. Quoted in David Katz, "Video Games and Obesity: Addiction or Entertainment?," Help Cure Childhood Obesity, November 3, 2013. www.helpcurechildobesity.com/video-games-and-obesity.html.

12. Quoted in Mike Snider, "Research: Video Games Help with Creativity in Boys and Girls," *Game Hunters* (blog), *USA Today*, November 2, 2011. http://content.usatoday.com/communities/gamehunters/post/2011/11/research-video-games-help-with-creativity/1#.Utw79bROnIU.

13. Quoted in *Sun* (London), "Video Games Make Us Better People; Cyber Warriors' Joy," February 1, 2013, p. 8.

14. Randolf Palmaira, "Welcome to Cybertherapy: Virtual Rehab Improves Patient Results," *Long-Term Living*, January 1, 2011. www.ltlmagazine.com/article/welcome-cybertherapy?page=2.

Chapter 4: Should Violent Video Games Be Regulated?

15. Anonymous blogger, "Should Violent Video Games be Banned: Yes!," Debate.org, www.debate.org/opinions/should-violent-video-games-be-banned.

16. John Hinderaker, "Should Violent Video Games Be Banned?," *Powerline*, January 11, 2013. www.powerlineblog.com/archives/2013/01/should-violent-video-games-be-banned.php.

17. Congressman Jim Matheson: 4th Congressional District of Utah, "Matheson Introduces H.R.287, the Video Games Ratings Enforcement Act," January 22, 2013. http://matheson.house.gov/index.cfm?sectionid=49&itemid=465.

18. Federal Trade Commission, "FTC Issues Report on Marketing Violent Entertainment to Children," April 12, 2007. www.ftc.gov/opa/2007/04/marketingviolence.shtm.

19. Fernando Trujano, "Why Violent Video Games Should Not Be Banned," Yahoo Contributor Network, April 24, 2010. http://voices.yahoo.com/why-violent-video-games-notbanned-5873058.html.

20. Quoted in Nadia Oxford, "ESRB Ratings: Do They Work?," *Game Theory*, September 21, 2010. http://gametheoryonline.com/2010/09/21/video-game-ratings-esrb-violence-mature.

21. Oxford, "ESRB Ratings: Do They Work?"

Glossary

advocates: Those who approve of something, such as a violent video game.

counterargument: The other side of an argument.

ethics: Rules of behavior based on ideas about what is morally good and bad.

first-person perspective: When gamers play the game through the eyes of the main character. They "see" through the character's eyes. In first-person shooter games, players look down the barrel of the main character's gun as though they are aiming the weapon themselves.

logic: A reasonable way of thinking about or understanding something.

logical fallacies: Errors in logical thinking.

scare tactic: When you use fear to influence an argument.

slippery slope: A logical fallacy whereby someone makes a claim that once a certain process or series of events has begun, it will lead to worse or more difficult things.

testimonial: Using the testimony, or statement, of a person as proof of the rightness of an argument.

Bibliography

Books

Neil Andersen, *At the Controls: Questioning Video and Computer Games*. Mankato, MN: Capstone, 2007. This title is designed to he readers critique video games as a medium and understand the motives behind the production of this popular form of entertainment.

Diane Marczely Gimpel, *Violence in Video Games*. Minneapolis, MN Core Library, 2013. This book asks readers to think critically and evaluate other points of view about video game violence.

Periodicals

Katie L. Burke, "Interface Facts: Video Games Allow People All over the World to Do Scientific Research," *American Scientist*, November–December 2012. Encouraged by the popularity of online games, scientists have created Internet sites such as Zooniverse to inspire citizen science projects.

Pamela Paul, "Reading, Writing and Video Game,." *New York Times*, March 17, 2013. This article explores the pros and cons of the use of educational computer games in the classroom.

Randall Stross, "'Exergames' Don't Cure Young Couch Potatoes," *New York Times*, June 24, 2012. Despite the promise from the gaming industry that exergames would get kids up and moving, this author notes studies that find they do not produce the increase in physical activity expected.

Websites

Are Video Games Bad for Me? KidsHealth
(http://kidshealth.org/kid/talk/qa/video_gaming.html). KidsHealth provides a forum for kids to find information about health, behavior, and development from before birth through the teen years.

Effects of Video Games, Buzzle
(www.buzzle.com/articles/effects-of-video-games). This interactive and colorful website provides numerous links to articles discussing a wide variety of issues related to video games.

Kids Ahead
(www.kidsahead.com). Video Game Revolution, PBS (www.pbs.org/kcts/videogamerevolution/impact/myths.html). PBS provides a broad overview of video games in this interactive site.

Index

About the Author

Hayley Mitchell Haugen is an associate professor of English at Ohio University Southern, where she teaches creative writing, American literature, and composition. In addition to writing and publishing poetry, creative essays, and literary criticism, she has published numerous nonfiction books for young readers.